D1161444

Hold My Paw

by

Jeremiah Dane

illustrated by Andreea Cauta

ISBN: 978-0-578-38338-5

Published 2022

Dedication:

As we drifted off to distant shores
I fell asleep with my hand in yours
And when I awake, I hope to find
our hands with fingers still intertwined

The ocean is big and I'm glad I have you
To share it all with and enjoy the view

Without you it wouldn't be as much fun
Swimming and laying out in the sun.

The ocean is big and I am quite small

I can't imagine ever seeing it all.

Tomorrow can we please play some more?

There are so many places I want to explore.

The ocean is big and there's so much to do.
I've had a lot of fun playing with you.

The sun is going down and I already ate.
Now I'm getting sleepy and it's getting late.

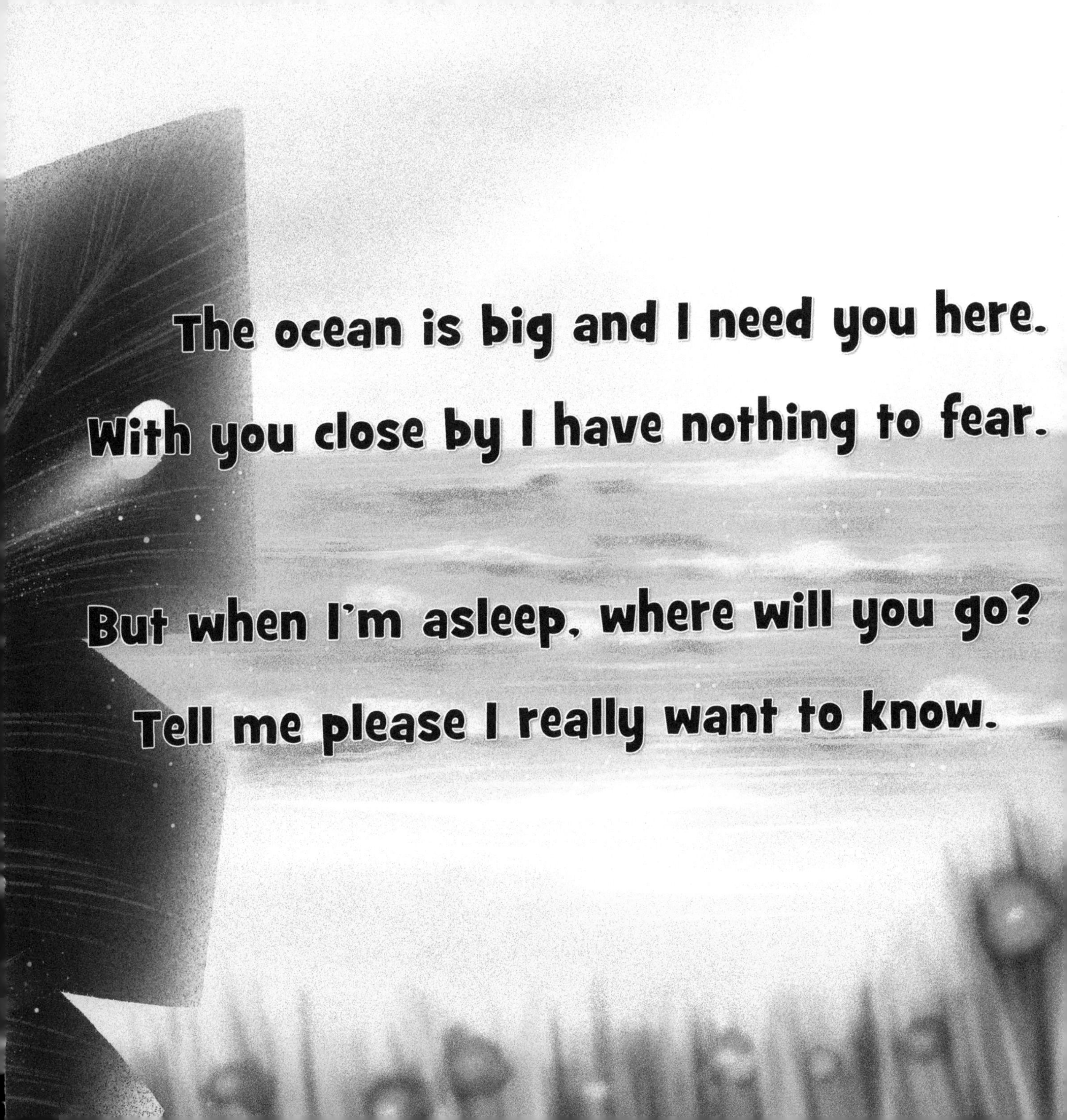

The ocean is big and I need you here.
With you close by I have nothing to fear.

But when I'm asleep, where will you go?
Tell me please I really want to know.

The ocean is big, as big as the sky.
While I am asleep, will you stay close by?

I feel so safe with you by my side,
And I'm afraid I might get caught in the tide.

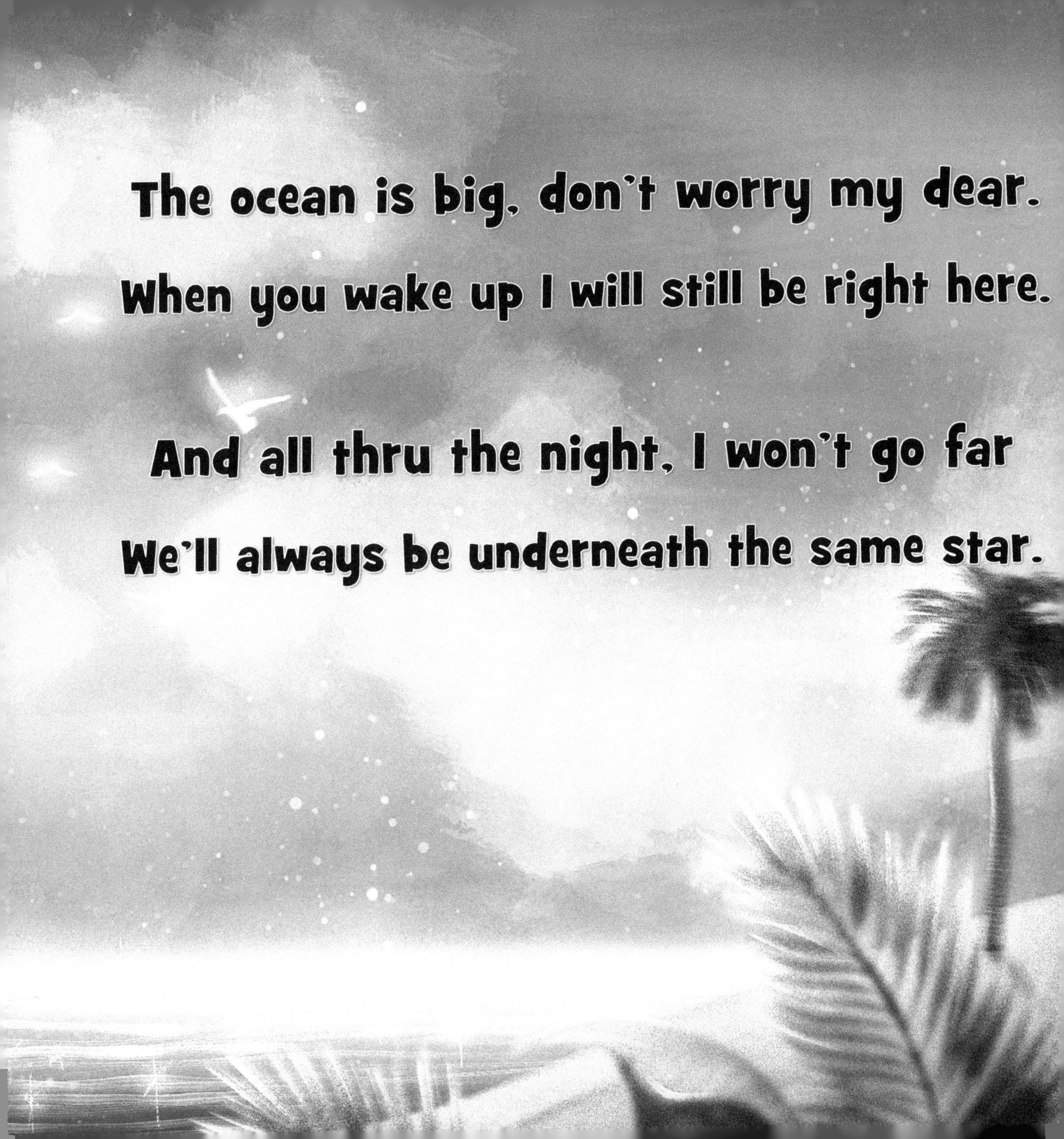

The ocean is big, don't worry my dear.
When you wake up I will still be right here.

And all thru the night, I won't go far
We'll always be underneath the same star.

The ocean is big, hold my paw thru the night
So I can always keep you within my sight.
This way no matter which way we flow,
Wherever you are, I also will go.

The ocean is big, now close your eyes
And sleep until the sun starts to rise.

Dream about all the faces you'll see,
The treasures you'll find and places you'll be.

Hold my paw so we don't drift apart
Stay by my side and close to my heart.

And when you wake up, you won't have to call
Because I'll be right here, still holding your paw.

About the Author:

Jeremiah Dane is a Certified Life, Relationship, Health and Wellness Coach and published Author.
To learn more and see other books by Jeremiah Dane, visit:
www.TheJeremiahDane.com

CPSIA information can be obtained
at www.ICGtesting.com
Printed in the USA
LVHW072057291022
731899LV00008B/131